♡ Eva at the Beach ♡

Read more
OWL DIARIES books!

OWL DIARIES

♥ Eva at the Beach ♥

Rebecca
Elliott

BRANCHES

SCHOLASTIC INC.

For the Sandfords and
all our fun beach trips. — R.E.

Special thanks to Ed Myer for
his contributions to this book.

Copyright © 2021 by Rebecca Elliott

All rights reserved. Published by Scholastic Inc., *Publishers since 1920.*
SCHOLASTIC, BRANCHES, and associated logos are trademarks
and/or registered trademarks of Scholastic Inc.

The publisher does not have any control over and does not assume
any responsibility for author or third-party websites or their content.

No part of this publication may be reproduced, stored in a retrieval system,
or transmitted in any form or by any means, electronic, mechanical, photocopying,
recording, or otherwise, without written permission of the publisher.
For information regarding permission, write to Scholastic Inc.,
Attention: Permissions Department, 557 Broadway, New York, NY 10012.

This book is a work of fiction. Names, characters, places, and incidents are
either the product of the author's imagination or are used fictitiously, and any
resemblance to actual persons, living or dead, business establishments,
events, or locales is entirely coincidental.

Library of Congress Cataloging-in-Publication Data

Names: Elliott, Rebecca, author, illustrator.
Title: Eva at the beach / Rebecca Elliott.
Description: First edition. | New York : Branches/Scholastic Inc., 2021. |
Series: Owl diaries ; 14 | Summary: Eva is very excited about a beach vacation
with her family andbest friend Lucy, but her secret fear of swimming where there
might be hungry sharks could keep her from finding the legendary mermowls.
Identifiers: LCCN 2020024285 (print) | LCCN 2020024286 (ebook) | ISBN
9781338298796 (paperback) | ISBN 9781338298819 (library binding) |
ISBN 9781338298826 (ebook)
Subjects: CYAC: Owls—Fiction. | Beaches—Fiction. | Fear—Fiction. |
Swimming—Fiction. | Vacations—Fiction. | Diaries—Fiction.
Classification: LCC PZ7.E45812 Epj 2021 (print) | LCC PZ7.E45812 (ebook)
| DDC [Fic]—dc23
LC record available at https://lccn.loc.gov/2020024285
LC ebook record available at https://lccn.loc.gov/2020024286

10 9 8 7 6 5 4 3 2 1   21 22 23 24 25

Printed in China   62
First edition, February 2021

Edited by Katie Carella
Book design by Marissa Asuncion

E
E,R,
Elliott

♥ Table of Contents ♥

1

♡ Vacation Time! ♡

Hi Diary,

It's me, Eva Wingdale! I feel **FLAPPY-FABULOUS** because this week I'm going on VACATION to Flappington Beach!

I love:

Going on vacation

Swimsuits

Collecting seashells

Building
sandcastles

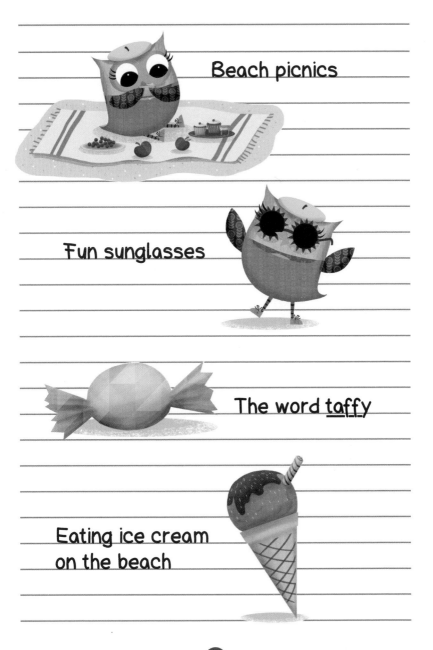

Beach picnics

Fun sunglasses

The word <u>taffy</u>

Eating ice cream
on the beach

I DO NOT love:

Missing my friends when I'm on vacation

Changing into my swimsuit

Jellyfish

Humphrey jumping on my sandcastles

4

Sand in my sandwich

Baby Mo burying my sunglasses

The word <u>crab</u>

Seagulls stealing my ice cream

This is my family on our last vacation. We always have such a **WING-CREDIBLE** time!

Humphrey

Mom

Dad

Me

Baby Mo

This is my pet bat, Baxter. He is excited, too, because while I'm away he gets to stay with Granny Owlberta and Grandpa Owlfred.

Being an owl is **OWLWAYS** fun, but especially on vacation.

We can fly super fast to wherever we want to go!

We stay in cool vacation tree houses.

We can see so much beautiful scenery with our big eyes.

We're asleep in the day and awake at night. We never get sunburned!

I live in a tree house on Woodpine Avenue in Treetopolis. My **BFF** (Best Feathery Friend), Lucy, lives next door.

The BEST thing about this family vacation is – Lucy's family is coming with us!

I will miss my other friends. But I'm going to take our class photo with me:

Lucy
Jacob
Hailey
Sue
Macy
Carlos
George
Lilly
Kiera
Zara
Mrs.
Me   Featherbottom
Zac

Tomorrow, Lucy and I will plan our trip. We head to the beach on Tuesday. I can't wait!

♡ Legend of the Mermowls ♡

Monday

Lucy came over tonight to help me pack for our vacation.

Yay! We're going to the beach!

How did you pack so quickly?!

Because, unlike you, I didn't pack <u>everything</u>!

Good point!

When I was showing Lucy my new sunglasses, Humphrey burst into my room. He took a photo of us with his new camera.

Brothers can be so annoying!

Lucy and I made a list of our beach plans. Here it is!

BEACH PLANS:

- Build sandcastles

- Make shell
  necklaces

- Eat ice cream

- Paint seashells

- Skim pebbles

- Swim in the sea

Diary, the truth is that I'm not <u>at all</u> excited about swimming in the sea.

I've actually always been scared of it. I know it sounds silly, which is why I've never told Lucy. But, Diary, there are all those big fish out there! What if one of them thinks I look tasty?

After I finished packing, Lucy stayed for a sleepover.

We got in bed early. (That way, our vacation starts sooner!)

I'm too excited to sleep!

Me too!

Dad came in to say good night.

You both need lots of sleep, so you can be ready to look for the <u>mermowls</u> of Flappington Beach tomorrow!

What is a mermowl?

Dad explained that **MERMOWLS** are half-fish half-owl creatures. They have feathers and a super shiny colorful fish tail.

Flappington Beach is famous for the Legend of the **MERMOWLS**! Owls say the **MERMOWLS** live far out to sea.

♡ I Can See the Sea! ♡

Tuesday

When we arrived at our vacation tree
house, we were so excited that we
started to sing!

Lucy and I were happy to share a room.

This vacation is going to be like one long sleepover!

We unpacked and flew to the beach.

Everyone went swimming, but I stayed on the sand.

As I watched everyone splashing about, I thought I saw something swimming really far out to sea. I wondered if it was a big, scary fish. I looked through Dad's binoculars. But what I saw was NOT a fish!

Lucy heard me and came running onshore. I told her what I saw.

I think I just saw a mermowl! I couldn't see clearly because it was so far out to sea. But I definitely saw something that looked feathery AND super shiny!

That's awesome! Let's see if we can see it again!

Yes! If we find it, we could be famous!

Later that night, Lucy and I went **MERMOWL** spotting. For a long time, we couldn't find anything. Then, just before sunrise, Lucy saw something.

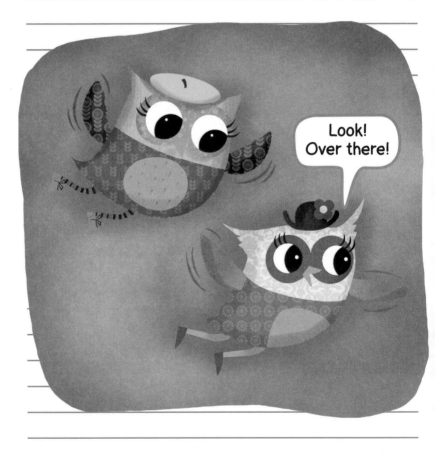

Look! Over there!

We could see TWO feathery, shiny
creatures somersaulting out of the water!

Those <u>must</u> be mermowls!

Let's get a better look!

We flew closer until, to our surprise . . .

It was SUE and HER MOM! They were wearing super shiny swimsuits! (Diary, I guess it wasn't a **MERMOWL** I saw earlier after all . . . It must have been Sue?!)

Hi, Eva and Lucy!

Hi! Are you vacationing here, too?!

Yes! We come here all the time.

We flew back to the beach together.

We made a campfire on the beach and ate marshmallows as the sun started to rise.

Sue, how did you learn to do those cool somersaults?

My mom taught me. She used to swim in the <u>Owlympics</u>.

I didn't want to tell Lucy or Sue that I was scared of big fish. I felt embarrassed. And I knew Sue would laugh at me. After all, even Baby Mo is happy swimming in the sea!

4

♥ Sandcastles and Secrets ♥

Wednesday

When we woke up, I told Lucy I didn't want to go swimming tonight.

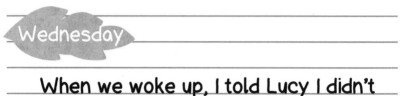

But you should still go swimming with Sue.

Why don't you want to come with us, Eva?

No reason. I really want to make a shell necklace. That's all.

32

I felt bad I didn't tell Lucy the <u>real</u> reason. I just felt so silly for feeling so scared.

Lucy is a super **BFF**.

Lucy and I had such a fun day!

We built
sandcastles.

We made shell necklaces.

We painted
seashells.

We skimmed pebbles.

AND . . .

We ate ice cream! It all got a bit messy, and then Humphrey took a photo of us!

Humphrey grabbed our list from my wing. He read it and started laughing.

Humphrey started pulling me toward the sea. I got scared.

My wings were shaking as I sat down on the sand.

I felt bad that my fear was spoiling Lucy's fun. So I told her the truth.

The thing is, Lucy . . . I'm scared to swim in the sea.

Just then, Sue turned up. She'd heard what I'd said!

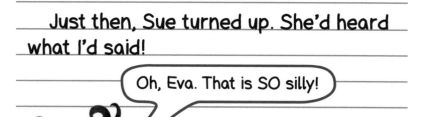

Oh, Eva. That is SO silly!

My cheeks went red and I flew off.

Eva, wait!

But I just kept flying.

I felt so embarrassed! I sat in a tree all night painting a seashell.

Finally, I flew back to the beach. Everyone was singing campfire songs.

It felt good to talk about what I was scared of, and to not have it be a secret anymore.

So why are you scared to swim in the sea, Eva?

It's just that there are lots of big fish out there. Like sharks.

Big fish aren't all scary. I know some super friendly dolphins. Would you like to meet them?

Sue's right, Eva. Meeting some big fish might help you not feel scared anymore.

Okay. Maybe that will work!

Oh, Diary. I'm happy Lucy and Sue want to help. But I'm still scared about meeting those big fish! I hope they don't want to eat me!

♡ Making a Splash! ♡

After breakfast, Lucy and I met Sue on the beach. She gave us new sparkly swimsuits that her mom had made!

I always feel less scared when I look fabulous!

We put them on.

Wow! These suits are great, Sue!

Yes! Thank you, Sue!

But I still
felt scared!

We flew out to sea until we saw a family of dolphins. The dolphins were big, but they were <u>so</u> friendly!

Hello, Sue!
Hello, Dolly! I've brought two friends to meet you all.
Eva, Lucy, meet Dolly, Fin, and Dave!

Fin did a huge somersault out of the water, splashing us and making us all laugh!

Soon, I didn't feel scared anymore.

Dolly, Dave, and Fin took us for a ride on their backs. We leapt out of the water. It was SUCH **FLAP-TASTIC** FUN!

I told the dolphins about how I'd been scared to meet them.

It seems silly now because you're so friendly!

I understand, Eva. I was scared of owls before I met Sue.

Then I saw a triangle sticking out of the water.

What's that over there?

Oh, that's just Terry the Shark.

THE WHAT???!

The shark swam over to us. Lucy and I shook with fear.

But then Terry spoke in a really kind voice!

I was still a bit worried that he might be hungry – and it turned out he was! But he didn't want to eat <u>us</u>.

We swam to a rock pool and ate sandwiches. They were delicious (though a bit soggy).

Who knew big fish were so friendly?! Now I'm sad we're going home tomorrow! I wish we had more time to spend with our new friends.

♡ The Mermowls! ♡

Dear Diary,
    I can't believe our **OWLMAZING**
vacation is almost over.

    I am excited to see Baxter though!
I hope he wasn't too much trouble for
Granny Owlberta and Grandpa Owlfred.

Lucy, Sue, and I went for one last swim with Terry and the dolphins.

Then we all said our good-byes.

We packed our bags.

Just then, Sue burst into our room.
She was waving a newspaper.

Flappington Beach News

Mermowls Spotted Near Flappington Beach!

A secret photographer took this photo yesterday. It appears to be a photo of three sparkly <u>mermowls</u> swimming far out at sea! Scientists do not know what to think of this photo.

We couldn't believe what we were seeing! And I don't think Sue realized what the picture was <u>actually</u> of...

We jumped up and down.

At our final campfire on the beach, everyone was talking about the photo.

Lucy, Sue, and I decided not to tell anyone it was just us swimming with the dolphins – this would be our little secret!

When I took another look at the photo, I noticed a blue wing in the corner. That is when I realized who had taken it!

I found Humphrey building a sandcastle with Baby Mo.

Hey, Humphrey, have you taken any interesting photos lately?

Yes! And I thought you looked pretty good in it!

You knew it was us?!

Of course! I was trying to take a nice picture of you with your friends.

I'd wanted to say sorry for being mean. I shouldn't have tried to pull you into the sea.

Thank you.

But then I saw the blurry photo and realized your swimsuits made you look like mermowls! So I sent it to the newspaper. Now you're a mermowl, and I got a photo in the paper!

SO cool! Thanks, Humphrey!

Then it was time for us all to fly home.

Diary, I'm going to miss this place. But the good news is: Mom and Dad said we can come back again soon.

Maybe next time we'll find the real mermowls!
Oh, I know we will!
CLICK!
You do know they're not real though, right?
If you say so, Humphrey!

♡ Home Again ♡

Saturday

It's often nice to go away, but it's always nice to come home again. Especially when you have a cute pet bat at home!

I told Baxter about our beach adventure.

Baxter smiled when he saw that we didn't become famous **MERMOWL** spotters . . . We became famous **MERMOWLS**!

EVA! COME SEE WHAT BABY MO TOOK A PHOTO OF!!!

Humphrey is yelling for me. I'd better go because he sounds excited. Wouldn't it be funny if <u>Baby Mo</u> took a pic of a real **MERMOWL**?! See you soon, Diary!

Rebecca Elliott was a lot like Eva when she was younger: She loved making things and hanging out with her best friends. Now that Rebecca is older, not much has changed — except that her best friends now include her two sons, Benjy and Toby. She still loves making things, like stories, cakes, music, and paintings. But as much as she and Eva have in common, Rebecca cannot fly or turn her head all the way around. No matter how hard she tries.

Rebecca is the author of several picture books, the young adult novel PRETTY FUNNY, the UNICORN DIARIES early chapter book series, and the bestselling OWL DIARIES series.

OWL DIARIES

How much do you know about Eva at the Beach?

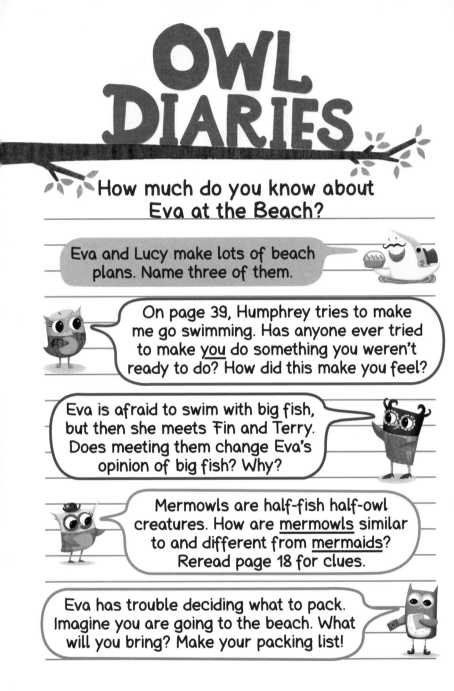

Eva and Lucy make lots of beach plans. Name three of them.

On page 39, Humphrey tries to make me go swimming. Has anyone ever tried to make <u>you</u> do something you weren't ready to do? How did this make you feel?

Eva is afraid to swim with big fish, but then she meets Fin and Terry. Does meeting them change Eva's opinion of big fish? Why?

Mermowls are half-fish half-owl creatures. How are <u>mermowls</u> similar to and different from <u>mermaids</u>? Reread page 18 for clues.

Eva has trouble deciding what to pack. Imagine you are going to the beach. What will you bring? Make your packing list!